Conrad

by Bill Schorr

A WALLABY BOOK
PUBLISHED BY POCKET BOOKS NEW YORK

Another *Original* publication of Wallaby Books

The cartoons in this book have been previously published in syndication.

A Wallaby Book published by
POCKET BOOKS, a division of Simon & Schuster, Inc
1230 Avenue of the Americas, New York, N.Y. 10020

ISBN: 0-671-50824-5

First Wallaby Books printing June, 1985

10 9 8 7 6 5 4 3 2 1

WALLABY and colophon are registered trademarks
of Simon & Schuster, Inc.

Printed in the U.S.A.

WAAAAHHH!

I'LL NEVER FIGURE OUT A SCHEME TO PAY OFF MY BOOKIE WITH THAT NOISE.

HEY, LADY... WHAT'S WRONG?

SNIFF... I'M A PRINCESS, BUT I CAN'T FIND A PRINCE TO MARRY...

...IN FAIRY TALES, A PRINCESS COULD KISS A FROG, HE'D TURN INTO A PRINCE AND THEY'D LIVE IN HER GOLDEN CASTLE...

A GOLDEN CASTLE.

PUCKER UP, MY SWEET LITTLE MEAL TICKET...

I FIGURED IF I WANTED TO MAKE THIS ENCHANTED PRINCE SCAM WORK, I NEEDED A CROWN...

...SO I BOUGHT THIS CHEAP BRASS ONE...

...IT TURNED MY SKIN GREEN.

SINCE YOU'RE AN ENCHANTED PRINCE AND I'M A PRINCESS, YOU'LL PROBABLY WANT TO (TEE-HEE) KISS ME.

WHOA! NO KISSING UNTIL AFTER WE'RE MARRIED...

SORRY, KID... BUT THOSE PALIMONY SUITS ARE PLAYING HECK WITH FAIRY TALES...

HUH?

FROGS HAVE WEBBED FLAT FEET...

...THAT'S HOW WE BEAT THE DRAFT.

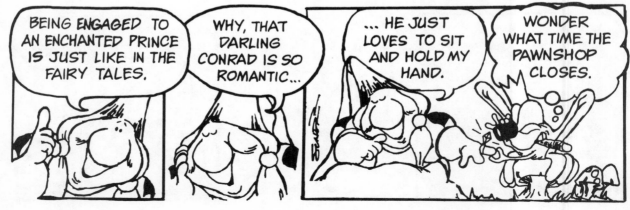

OH, AGATHA... DADDY DOESN'T WANT ME TO GET MARRIED... YOU'RE MY FAIRY GODMOTHER ...WHAT SHOULD I DO?

TELL YOUR FATHER YOU'RE A GROWN WOMAN FULLY CAPABLE OF MAKING YOUR OWN MATURE RESPONSIBLE DECISIONS CONCERNING MATTERS OF YOUR HEART...

THAT'S TERRIFIC... ANY MORE ADVICE?

YEAH... GET RID OF THE FROG... THEY MAKE LOUSY PETS!

I ALMOST GOT MARRIED ONCE...

WHY DIDN'T YOU?

HE DIDN'T APPROVE OF MY CAREER, SO HE CALLED OFF THE WEDDING.

HOW SAD... WHAT EVER HAPPENED TO HIM?

YOU'RE SITTING ON HIM...

IT SAYS HERE IF YOU WANT TO BE A PRINCE YOU HAVE TO SLAY A DRAGON, KILL A GIANT, OR KISS A PRINCESS.

HOW BIG'S THE GIANT?

AGGIE... CAN YOU GIVE ME SOMETHING TO MAKE ME MORE APPEALING TO CONRAD?

SURE... DRINK THIS...

WHAT'S IT DO?

IT TURNS YOU INTO A 150-POUND FLY!

ZAP!

AAAARRRRGGH!

NEVER EAT A LIGHTNING BUG WHILE STANDING IN A POOL OF WATER!

WHOM DO YOU WANT TO CONTACT FROM THE SPIRIT WORLD?

THE THREE WISE MEN.

SPLAT!

WOULD YOU SETTLE FOR THE THREE STOOGES?

OH, CONRAD...

HOPPY NEW YEAR! (TEE HEE)

TEE HEE HEE HEE--

GEE... I HATE ETHNIC HUMOR!

THIS YEAR I RESOLVE TO GIVE UP GAMBLING...

I'M SO PROUD OF YOU, CONRAD... I'LL BET YOU CAN DO IT...

YOU'RE ON!

THE PROBLEM WITH FROGS IS THEY ALL LOOK PRETTY MUCH ALIKE...

FOR INSTANCE, I DATED ONE LITTLE FROG FOR SIX MONTHS...

...BEFORE I FOUND OUT IT WAS MY COUSIN RALPH!

REMEMBER, YOU'RE NOT LOSING A DAUGHTER...YOU'RE GAINING A SON...

...I WANT YOU TO THINK OF ME AS THE SON YOU NEVER HAD...

...SO WHAT D'YA SAY, **DAD**... CAN I BORROW THE KEYS TO THE VAULT TONIGHT?

I MISS OZZIE NELSON...

WELL, AGGIE... I PUT THAT LOVE POTION YOU GAVE ME IN CONRAD'S MILK...

HEH HEH... HOW'D IT WORK?

NOT SO WELL...

SO TELL ME, BRIGHT EYES, DO YOU LIVE ALONE?

TODAY IS ROBERT E. LEE'S BIRTHDAY... AND I WANT YOU TO HELP ME CELEBRATE.

UH... SURE, KID... WHAT D'YA WANT ME T'DO?

SURRENDER...

ACCORDING TO THIS ARTICLE, BODY LANGUAGE IS ESSENTIAL TO EXPRESSING ONESELF.

NO HABLA ESPAÑOL.

I HEARD THOSE INSULTS AND INNUENDOES ABOUT ME MARRYING YOUR DAUGHTER...

...BUT NOTHING YOU SAY WILL CHANGE MY MIND.

OFF WITH HIS HEAD!

WITH THE POSSIBLE EXCEPTION OF THAT.

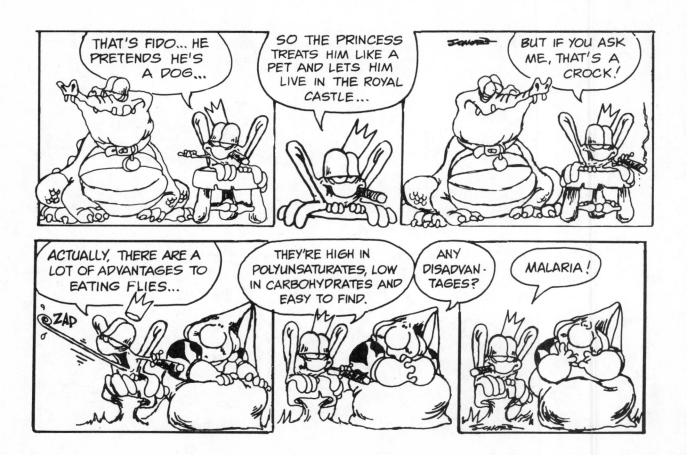

IN HONOR OF SUSAN B. ANTHONY'S BIRTHDAY, I WANT YOU TO PROMISE NEVER TO TREAT ME LIKE A SEX OBJECT...

OKAY.

WAAAAAH!

HI, MR. FROG... I'M LITTLE RED RIDING HOOD.

"HOOD?"

...WHERE'D YOU GET A NAME LIKE THAT, LITTLE GIRL?

GIMME YOUR WALLET.

OH....

THIS PERFUME COST $150 AN OUNCE, BUT IT'S WORTH EVERY PENNY BECAUSE IT'S GUARANTEED TO TURN MY BOYFRIEND INTO AN ANIMAL ...

ZAP!

NEVER MIND.

QUICK, AGGIE... MAKE ME IRRESISTIBLE TO CONRAD...

POOF!

LET ME REPHRASE THAT...

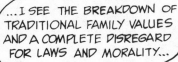

POOR CONRAD...

EVERY TIME HE GOES TO THE DOCTOR...

HIS TONGUE STICKS TO THE DEPRESSOR.

I FEEL TERRIBLE...

NO WONDER...

YOU CAUGHT A BUG... HA HA HA HA HA

FOUR OUT OF FIVE DOCTORS MAKE LOUSY COMEDIANS...

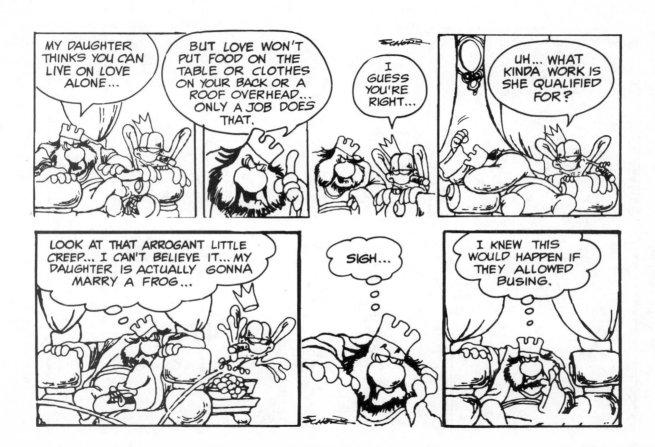

STAND BACK, DEARIE, WHILE I TURN THIS PUMPKIN INTO A COACH...

POOF

OK, LARDOS... 100 PUSH-UPS!

I COME FROM A LONG LINE OF ATHLETES. MY UNCLE MAX RAN IN THE BOSTON MARATHON...

OH?

YEP... MAX STARTED OUT FAR BEHIND THE REST OF THE PACK... BUT HE HUNG IN THERE...

AND HE FINISHED ON THE HEELS OF THE WINNER!

I'M IMPRESSED!

'COURSE IT TOOK TEN MINUTES TO SCRAPE HIM OFF...

AARG!

HMM... LET'S CHECK OUT THIS MONTH'S CENTERFOLD...

WOW!...WILL YA LOOK AT THAT BOD AND THOSE LEGS... WHEW!

SIGH

I LOVE FIELD AND STREAM.

TELL ME, DARLING... WHAT'S YOUR FAVORITE PART OF A PICNIC? THE YUMMY FOOD, THE FRESH AIR, OR (TEE HEE) THE CHARMING COMPANY?

ZAP!

THE FLIES...

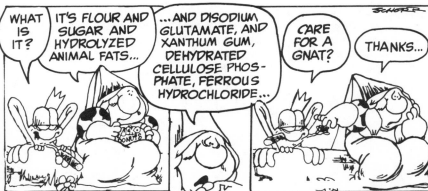

WHAT'D YA KNOW, A GLOWWORM.

SHINE LITTLE GLOWWORM... GLIMMER... GLIMMER...

YOU MAKE A TERRIFIC DINNER... DINNER...

ZAP!

I LOVE THE MILLS BROTHERS.

IT'S A LETTER FROM MY AUNT HARRIET IN CALIFORNIA ...

... SEEMS MY UNCLE MARVIN BOUGHT HIMSELF A GIANT HOT TUB...

... AND NOW...

... SHE'S STUCK WITH 800 GALLONS OF FROG SOUP.

HA!... YOU DON'T HONESTLY EXPECT ME TO BELIEVE YOU REALLY LOOK LIKE TOM SELLECK... DO YOU?

WHY NOT?

BE SERIOUS, FLYBREATH... THE MAN'S 6'4" TALL...

HEY, NO PROBLEM...

NOW... OF COURSE... YOU'LL HAVE TO IMAGINE THE MUSTACHE AND HAIRY CHEST...

THIS IS THE 80'S, CONRAD... AND ACCORDING TO THIS, THE KEY TO A MODERN 80'S TYPE RELATIONSHIP IS HONESTY.

IN THAT CASE...

REMEMBER HOW I TOLD YOU I REALLY LOOK LIKE BURT REYNOLDS... WELL, IT'S NOT TRUE.

IT'S NOT?

I REALLY LOOK LIKE TOM SELLECK.

TOM SELLECK! EEEEEEE!

I LIKE TO CHANGE WITH THE TIMES...

THIS STRIP'S A HELLUVA LOT EASIER TO DRAW SINCE I BECAME INVISIBLE...

THE 'STEALTH FROG' STRIKES AGAIN...